GRANDMA'S PEAR TREE

WRITTEN BY SUZANNE SANTILLAN

ILLUSTRATED BY ATILIO PERNISCO

To my family and friends, thanks for helping me make a dream come true. ❧ SS

I dedicate this book to all the children I know—the kids from Coolidge, Child's Garden, the Pasqualers, the Miclat kids, Alex, Briana, Seba, Claudita, Andrew, Gabriel, and Anthony. And, most importantly, my own and dearest Camilu. ❧ AP

Text ©2010 Suzanne Santillan
Illustration ©2010 Atilio Pernisco

Santillan, Suzanne.

Grandma's pear tree / written by Suzanne Santillan; illustrated by Atilio Pernisco;
—1 ed. —McHenry, IL : Raven Tree Press, 2010.

p.;cm.

SUMMARY: A ball gets stuck in Grandma's pear tree and
everyone in the family tries to help get it back.

English-only Edition
ISBN 978-1-934960-82-0 hardcover

Bilingual Edition
ISBN 978-1-934960-80-6 hardcover
ISBN 978-1-934960-81-3 paperback

Audience: pre-K to 3rd grade
Title available in English-only or bilingual English-Spanish editions

1. Family/Multigenerational—Juvenile fiction. 2. Lifestyles/
Country Life—Juvenile fiction. I. Illust. Pernisco, Atilio. II. Title.

LCCN: 2009931226

Printed in Taiwan
10 9 8 7 6 5 4 3 2 1
First Edition

Raven Tree Press
A Division of Delta Systems Co., Inc.
www.raventreepress.com

Free activities for this book are available at www.raventreepress.com

PRINTED WITH
SOY INK

GRANDMA'S PEAR TREE

written by SUZANNE SANTILLAN

illustrated by ATILIO PERNISCO

"Grandpa, I need your help! Grandpa, the ball is stuck in the pear tree. I was playing a game. When I bounced the ball too hard, it flew up in the tree. I promised Grandma that I'd stay away from her tree. If I tell Grandma it's up there, she'll be very cross."

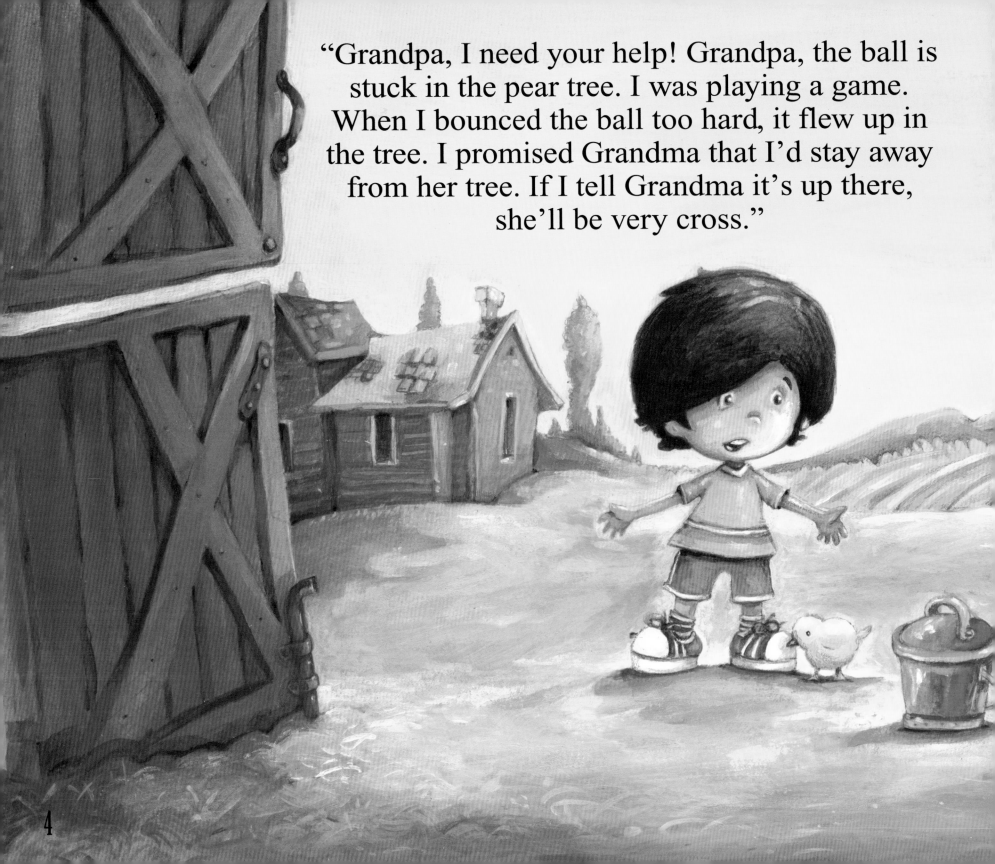

"I must finish milking the cow," Grandpa replied. "Throw your shoe at it. The shoe may get it down. When I'm done milking the cow, I will help you."

Jessie walked up to Grandma's pear tree and threw his shoe…

"Oh no!"

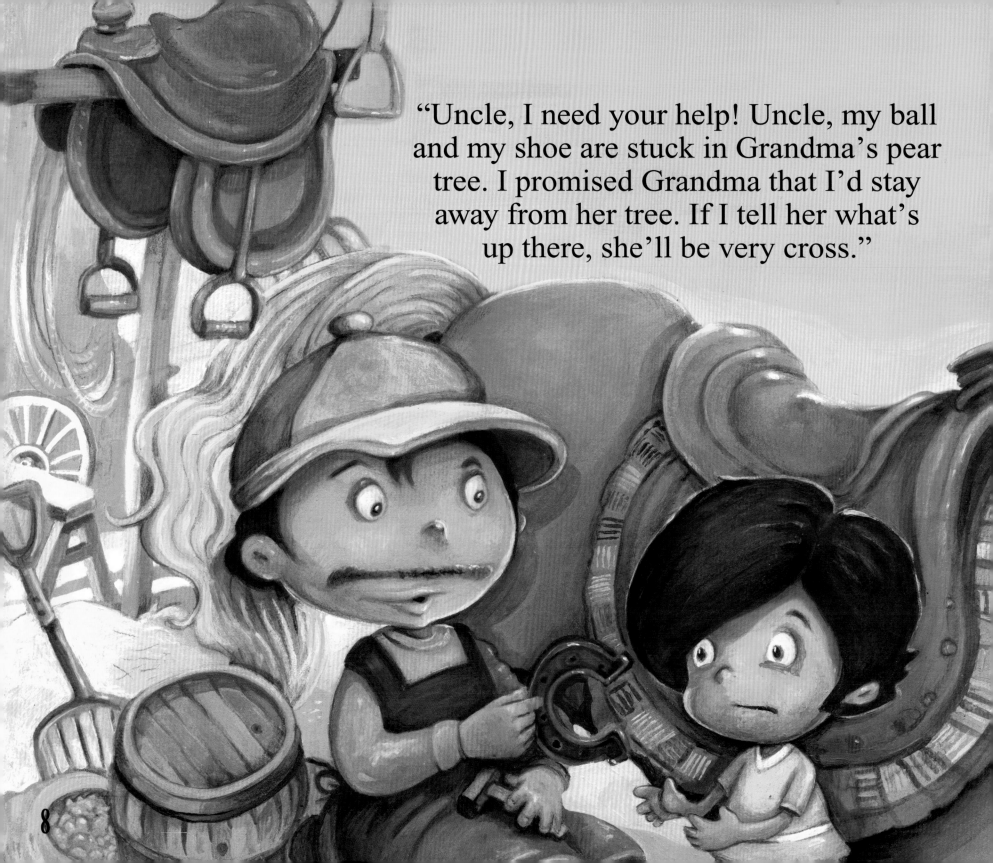

"Uncle, I need your help! Uncle, my ball and my shoe are stuck in Grandma's pear tree. I promised Grandma that I'd stay away from her tree. If I tell her what's up there, she'll be very cross."

8

"The horse needs a
new shoe," Uncle replied.
"Use the broom. The broom
may get them down.

When I'm done
shoeing the horse,
I will help you."

9

Jessie walked up to
Grandma's pear tree and
raised the broom…

"Oh no!"

"Cousin, I need your help! Cousin,
my ball, my shoe and the broom
are stuck in Grandma's pear tree.

I promised Grandma that I'd stay away from her tree.
If I tell her what's up there, she'll be very cross."

"The goat has escaped from
his pen," Cousin replied.
"Use the chicken.

The chicken will fly in the tree
and knock your things down.
When I've caught the goat,
I will help you."

Jessie walked up to Grandma's pear tree and tossed the chicken…

14

"Oh no!"

15

"Sister, I need your help! Sister, the chicken, the broom,
my shoe, and my ball are stuck in Grandma's pear tree.
I promised Grandma that I'd stay away from her tree.
If I tell her what's up there, she'll be very cross."

"The donkey needs water and food," Sister replied.
"Use the cat. The cat will scare the chicken.
The flapping and squawking will knock your things down.
When I am done feeding the donkey, I will help you."

Jessie brought the cat to Grandma's pear tree.
He climbed to a very tall branch…
and lay down to sleep.

18

"Oh no!"

"Grandma, I'm sorry. I broke my promise to you.
But it all started with the ball…"

"Oh little one, I'm not cross with you," Grandma replied. "Family is more important than even my tree."

21

"I have an idea," said Grandma as she looked at the things stuck up in her tree.

22

"Let's get the ladder. The ladder is very heavy, but if you help me, we can lift it together."

Grandma climbed up to the top of her tree and started dropping the things down.

Down walked the cat as calm as can be.

Down flew the chicken.

25

Down dropped the broom.

Down came my shoe.

Down bounced the ball.

Down fell the ladder with a thud on the ground...

27

"Oh my!"

28

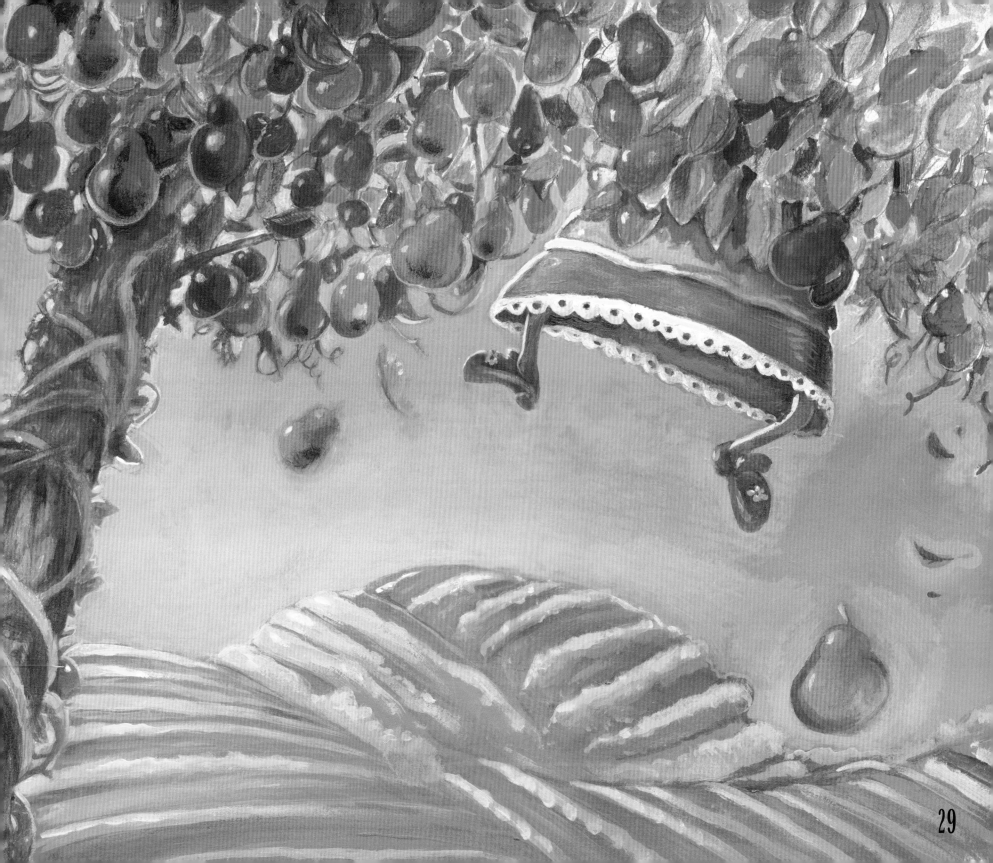

"Everyone, come quickly! Now Grandma is stuck in her tree!"